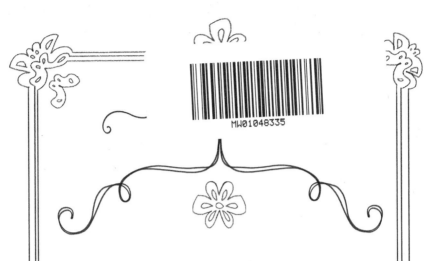

The Complete
Brontë Sisters
Children's Collection

Charlotte, Emily and Anne Brontë

Published by Sweet Cherry Publishing Limited
Unit 36, Vulcan House,
Vulcan Road,
Leicester, LE5 3EF
United Kingdom

First published in the UK in 2022
2022 edition

2 4 6 8 10 9 7 5 3 1

ISBN: 978-1-78226-708-9

The Complete Brontë Sisters Children's Collection:
Agnes Grey

Based on the original story by Anne Brontë,
adapted by Stephanie Baudet.

Cover design by Arianna Bellucci and Amy Booth
Illustrations by Arianna Bellucci

Lexile® code numerical measure L = Lexile® 710L

www.sweetcherrypublishing.com

Printed and bound in Turkey
T.OP005

Agnes Grey

Anne Brontë

Sweet Cherry

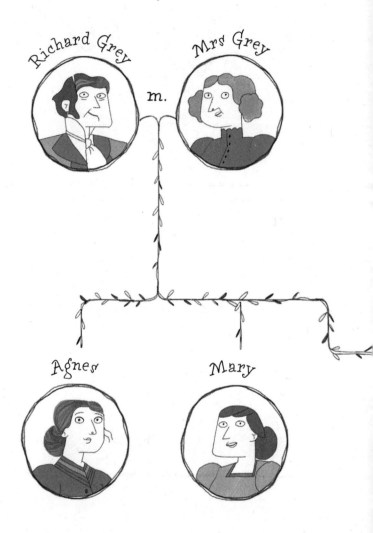

Babies who died in infancy

Chapter One

My mother was advised not to
marry my father. He was a church
minister, and not rich enough
for her to have the comfortable
life she was used to. Her father
disapproved, and said that if they

married, he would leave her nothing in his will.

But my mother said that she would rather live in a cottage with my father, Richard Grey, than in a palace with anyone else.

My sister, Mary, and I were the only ones to survive of the six children that our parents had. We were a very happy family despite having little money. There were many people far worse off.

But my father always felt bad that he couldn't give my mother the things she was used to. A friend suggested that, to earn a lot of money, he should buy a shipload of goods to sell in a foreign country. When the ship sank, we lost everything.

We were poorer now. We sold our pony and cart. We mended our clothes many times instead of buying new ones, and we had only one candle in the house instead of two.

I didn't mind being poor, but I wanted to help. One day I said, 'I would like to be a governess and look after and teach children.' I thought I could give the money I earned to my family.

Mamma laughed. 'You? A governess! You are dreaming, Agnes.'

She didn't realise that I was now eighteen and not a child anymore.

'Surely I could teach little ones? I love children,' I said.

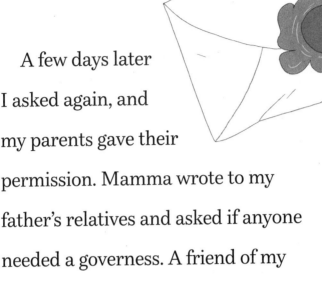

A few days later
I asked again, and
my parents gave their
permission. Mamma wrote to my
father's relatives and asked if anyone
needed a governess. A friend of my
aunt's, called Mrs Bloomfield, was
willing to give me the job.

I was so excited! I was to go out
into the world, act for myself and
earn my own living! I would show
my family that I was not helpless.

Chapter Two

It was several weeks before I left. I was sad whenever I did anything for the last time. My last ramble on the moors, my last stroke of our pet pigeons. My last tune on the piano and my last song for Papa.

Then came the last time I would
share the room with my sister, Mary.

The next day I tried to be cheerful
and excited, but deep down I
was scared. We had hired a small
carriage for the journey, and as I
climbed into it next to the driver, I

pulled the veil over my face so no one could see me crying.

As we climbed the hill I looked back. There was the church spire and our grey house beside it, lit up by a beam of sunshine. The rest of the village was still in shadow.

About noon we reached Wellwood House. We drove through the tall iron gates and up the smooth drive with green lawns either side. I was shaking with nerves.

The house was large and new.
It stood in a small wood of tall
poplar trees.

The maid showed
me in, and I met Mrs
Bloomfield. She was
tall and slim with
thick black hair,
cold grey eyes and
yellowish skin.

She watched me
eat a small meal

that had been kept for me, then said I should meet the children.

'My son, Tom, is seven. He is the best of them all,' she said. 'He needs to be guided, but he always speaks the truth. Mary Ann is six and will need watching, but she is a very good little girl. She will sleep in your room. Fanny is four and Harriet is two, and they will stay in the nursery with the nurse.'

Mr Bloomfield m. Mrs Bloomfield   Uncle Robson

Tom   Mary Ann

Harriet   Fanny

18

At that moment, the children came in. Tom was a big boy with blond hair and blue eyes. Mary Ann was also tall, but had dark hair like her mother.

They seemed like bold, lively children and I hoped we would soon be friends.

They took me to see the schoolroom that Tom insisted was *his*. He dragged the rocking horse into the middle of the room, and showed me how well he could ride.

'I hope you won't use the spurs and whip like that on a real pony,' I said.

'I certainly will!' he said.

'It's my horse too,' said Mary
Ann, approaching it.

Tom lifted his fist menacingly.

'Surely you wouldn't hit your
sister, Tom?' I said.

'I have to sometimes, to keep her
in order,' he said.

We went out into the garden and
he showed me some traps on the
lawn. 'They're for birds,' he said.

'That's very wicked!' I said.
'Birds can feel pain too.'

'But *I* can't feel it,' he said. 'Papa says he used to do the same things when he was a boy.'

During dinner Mr Bloomfield complained and criticised everything. One day, the meat was overdone, another, it was cut wrongly. No matter what it was, he always blamed it on his wife. It made me feel awkward.

I soon found out that the children were impossible to keep

in order. They did exactly as they wanted, and their mother would not listen to anything I said.

I had to catch my pupils and drag them to the table. They refused to do their lessons.

Mary Ann would often roll on the floor and go limp if I tried to pick her up. She would lie like that until dinner time, then give me a grin of triumph as she ran out of the room.

I argued, coaxed, threatened and pleaded. But nothing worked.

Sometimes Mary Ann shrieked loudly until her mother came running. I always got the blame. Her mother would fix her cold, stony eyes on me and then walk away.

In the mornings Mary Ann would often refuse to wash or dress, and screamed if I tried to brush her hair.

When at last little Fanny came into the schoolroom, I hoped she would be better behaved. But she wasn't. She would spit in my face or bellow like a bull if she didn't get her own way.

It was not at all like I had imagined.

At last it was Christmas, and I went home for a wonderful two weeks with my family.

Chapter Three

When I returned to Wellwood
House I was determined to do
better. One snowy day in January all
three children said they were going
to be naughty. I tried everything I
could to talk them out of it.

'Mary Ann, throw Miss Grey's desk out of the window!' said Tom.

I looked at him with horror. All my belongings were in my desk, and we were three floors up.

I managed to save my desk. Then, all three children ran outside into the snow. They laughed and shouted. I knew that if their mother saw them behaving in such a way, without their hats, gloves and boots, I would be in terrible trouble.

But it was Mr Bloomfield who
appeared. He shouted at me to get
them inside.

'I can't, sir,' I said. 'You must call them yourself, please. They won't listen to me.'

'Come in, you filthy brats, or I'll horsewhip you!' he roared. They obeyed.

Sometimes their father would pop his head inside the schoolroom as his children were eating. He would find them spilling milk over the table, plunging their fingers into each other's mugs, or fighting about the food.

Then he would tell me off for not teaching them better behaviour.

I spent a lot of time clearing up the mess after them. One day I threatened no supper until they had tidied up, and Tom flew into a rage. He scattered the bread and milk over the table, hit his sisters, kicked the coal out of the fire and tried to tip the table and chairs over.

I grabbed him and held him, kicking and yelling, until Mary Ann fetched their mother. All she did was ask the maid to bring more supper and to tell me to clear up the mess.

When their Uncle Robson came to stay, he laughed when they were naughty, and even praised them.

The children pestered any guests at the house by climbing on their knees or searching through their pockets to see what they could find. They begged for presents.

Mrs Bloomfield was annoyed by this but expected me to deal with it.

One warm evening near the end of May, when I thought I had finally made some progress with my pupils, Mrs Bloomfield told me that I was dismissed. I had lost my job. She said that I hadn't been strict enough and that although her children were very bright, they hadn't learnt much from me.

I was sent home. I hadn't even kept my job for a year, and I felt like a failure.

My family never said, 'I told you so'. They were all pleased to see me, and knew I tried my best.

Mamma said that I was paler and thinner than before I left for Wellwood House. She was worried

about my health. I spent several months recovering from my ordeal.

Soon the little money I had saved had been spent on helping my family. I decided to look for another job.

I looked for adverts in the newspapers, but Mamma was never impressed by them. She said that they did not pay enough, or that my duties would be too much.

Finally, I put an advert in the paper myself.

Governess looking for a position at
fifty pounds a year. Able to teach
music, French, Latin and German.
Please reply to: Miss Agnes Grey,
The Parsonage, Hamley, Yorks.

Two people replied, but only one
was willing to pay the sum I had
asked for. This was the family of Mr
Murray, of Horton Lodge, about
seventy miles from our village. I had
never been more than twenty miles
from home in my life.

I guessed that Mr Murray was very rich and important. I hoped he would treat me with respect, not like a servant.

My pupils were older and I hoped they would be better behaved than the last ones.

The 31st of January was a wild day with a strong wind. Snow whirled through the air. Despite the weather, I was determined to go.

Chapter Four

My journey took much longer than it should have. It was dark by the time I reached the railway station. Mr Murray's servant met me with a small carriage and drove me to Horton Lodge.

The cold, sharp snow drifted around us and filled my lap.

At last we stopped outside the porch of a large house with long windows down to the ground.

I expected to be met by Mr or Mrs Murray, but instead there was a man dressed in black. He took me along a passage and showed me into the schoolroom.

Four people were there. Two young ladies and two young gentlemen. After greeting me, the older girl looked at her sister and said, 'Matilda, take a candle and show her to her room.'

Miss Matilda was a big girl of about fourteen. She pulled a face, but picked up a candle and led me up the back stairs through a long, narrow passage. We reached a

small but comfortable room. She offered me tea or coffee, and said she would ask the maid to bring it.

I took off my heavy wet cloak, shawl, bonnet and gloves. The servant arrived with my drink and put it on the chest of drawers.

I sat down in front of the smouldering fire to drink my tea and eat the thin piece of bread and butter that had come with it. It was the first thing I'd eaten since breakfast.

At last, my luggage was brought up. I changed into my nightclothes and went to bed.

I had a strange feeling the next day as I pulled up my blind and looked out at the unknown world.

It was a wide, white wilderness. Snow covered the ground and weighed down the trees.

I had made the mistake at the Bloomfield's of calling the children by their first names. Here I needed to remember to use Miss and Master when speaking to them.

I went downstairs to meet the family.

Mr Murray was a blustering country landowner who liked to

hunt foxes. He was a tall, heavy-set

gentleman with red cheeks and a

red nose. I only ever saw him on

Sundays at church, but I would often hear him laughing loudly or swearing at one of the servants.

Mrs Murray was a good-looking lady of forty. I found out that she loved hosting parties and liked to wear the very latest fashions.

I didn't meet her until after eleven o'clock on that first morning, which my mother would have thought very rude. She told me that she wanted the girls to be attractive, and while she wanted them to learn, they should not be made to work too hard. With the two boys, I should teach them Latin grammar so they could go to the best schools.

'John is a little high-spirited and Charles a little nervous,' she said. 'But, Miss Grey, *you* must keep your temper and be patient. Make them as happy as you can and you will do very well.'

Rosalie was sixteen, and a very graceful girl. She was tall and slender with exquisite fair hair,

which she wore in ringlets. I wish I could say that her personality was as beautiful as her face.

She was cold, scornful and cheeky at the beginning, although that improved with time.

Neither she nor her brothers and sister had ever been taught right from wrong. They had always been allowed to do just what they wanted. They had not been taught to think of others and not to be greedy.

Matilda was fourteen and had darker hair than her sister. She was a big, heavy-boned girl, who did not care about her looks. She also did not care about learning anything. She wasted a lot of time. Once, when I mentioned this, her mother told me that, if I wanted to keep my job, I must let Matilda do what she wanted.

I was shocked that she had learnt to swear horribly from her father. I tried to tell her how awful it sounded coming from a young lady, but she just laughed and blamed her father.

Away from lessons she was happy. She loved to ride her pony and play with the dogs.

John was eleven when I arrived. He was a healthy boy, mostly honest and good-natured, although very rough and disruptive. He was very unteachable, but to my relief, was soon sent away to school.

Master Charles was ten and much

smaller than John. He was quite a

cowardly and selfish little boy, and always up to mischief. He refused to learn and still could not read at the end of the two years I spent there.

I ate all my meals with my pupils in the schoolroom, whenever they wanted them. Sometimes they would stay in bed late in the morning, and I had to wait for my breakfast until I was almost faint with hunger.

They had their lessons when and where they wanted, too – early, late, outside, inside. I had no say in the matter, and often caught colds sitting on the damp grass.

The parents and the children treated me with little to no respect. The servants did the same, even though I often stood up for them against the children.

I soon learnt that a governess was invisible and unimportant.

Chapter Five

Once the boys were at school, I very slowly made some progress with the girls.

When Rosalie reached eighteen her mother decided to hold a ball for her. She was now a young woman.

It was time for her to be presented to everyone of any importance in the hope of finding a husband.

One day, about a month before the ball, she sat on a stool in front of me as I was reading a letter from home.

'Stop reading that boring letter, Miss Grey. I want to talk about the ball,' she said. 'You must put off your holiday until it is over.'

'But why?' I said. 'I shall not be at the ball.'

'You must see me in my new dress! I shall be so pretty that you will worship me.'

'I can't bear the thought of not being at home for Christmas,' I said. 'My sister is getting married.'

She scoffed when I told her about my sister's future husband, because he was not rich and handsome. She didn't think the qualities of being good, wise and kind were important.

I took my holiday as planned. When I returned, both Rosalie and Matilda fought for my attention.

'I will tell you about the ball,' said Rosalie.

'Hold your tongue!' shouted Matilda. 'I want to tell her about my new mare.'

'Be quiet, Matilda!'

At last Rosalie gave in because her sister had the loudest voice. I heard all about the new horse and how amazingly well Matilda rode it, and what courage she had.

'I could easily have jumped a five-barred gate,' she said.

'Oh, Matilda, what stories you are telling,' said Rosalie.

'Well, I *could* have.'

Then it was Rosalie's turn.

I heard all about the ball – the decorations, the supper, the music and the guests. 'You must see my dress tomorrow,' she exclaimed. 'It's white gauze over pink satin and I wore a necklace and bracelet of beautiful big pearls!'

She then told me about the men who had paid attention to her and the wives she had made jealous.

My head was spinning when she finally stopped talking twenty minutes later.

On Sunday we went to church as usual. Afterwards Miss Rosalie said, 'Well, Miss Grey. What do you think of Mr Weston, the new curate?'

'I don't know. I liked his style of reading, when he read from the Bible.'

'You saw him, didn't you?'

'Yes,' I said. 'But I can't judge a person by one look at their face.'

That afternoon the two girls visited the poor people on their father's estate, as they sometimes did. Once or twice I went with them, and sometimes I went on my own.

The girls always looked down on the poor. They never tried to imagine what life was like for them. Sometimes they would watch the family eating their meals, and make rude remarks about their food. Often they would laugh at what they said.

I heard that Mr Weston often visited the poor villagers, talked to them and gave advice. He listened to their problems, and helped them when he could.

I began to enjoy Sundays very much. At church we would hear Mr Weston speak. He made the sermons interesting and meaningful.

He was of average height and had a square face and dark brown hair. Under his dark eyebrows, his brown eyes were full of expression. There was something about his mouth that showed he was a determined man.

I judged him to be a truly kind and gentle man.

Chapter Six

One day, one of the villagers was

worried because her cat was missing.

I told her I would help look for it.

As I was leaving, Mr Weston came

through the door with the cat in his

arms. It was the first time I had seen

him smile, and it was very pleasant.

Another day we were walking back from church and, as usual, no one was talking to me. The sun was warm and the larks sang sweetly. I began to look in the hedgerows for some familiar flower that would remind me of home.

I spotted three lovely primroses nestled in the roots of an old oak

tree, but they were too far up the bank to reach.

I was about to turn away when I heard footsteps behind me. A well-known voice said, 'Let me reach them for you, Miss Grey.'

It was Mr Weston.

'The young ladies have left you alone,' he said, when he had given me the flowers.

'They prefer to talk to other people,' I said.

So we walked together. He asked me what my favourite flowers were.

'Primroses, bluebells and heather,' I said.

'Not violets?'

'No, because there are none of those at home.'

'You are lucky to have a home, Miss Grey,' he said. 'Even if you hardly ever visit it. I do not have one.'

'But I'm sure there is happiness in your life,' I said.

He nodded. 'Oh, I am happy now, because I can be useful and help people.'

We were seen by Rosalie, who teased me later.

'Ha ha, Miss Grey! No wonder you lingered so far behind!'

'Nonsense!' I said with a laugh.

But I kept two of the primroses until they had withered. The other

one, I pressed between the pages of my Bible.

Rosalie began seeing the vicar, Mr Hatfield. She said he amused her but she would never marry him because he did not earn enough money. I told her she was teasing him, but she ignored me. Other people's feelings did not matter to her. She just wanted to have fun.

It ended badly. She broke his heart. Then she seemed set on

coming between me and Mr
Weston. She couldn't resist trying
to show that he would choose her
over me. One day, when we were
walking together, she came and
took over our conversation. She
drew him away from me, smiling
sweetly up at him.

When Mr Weston turned
and tried to include me in the
conversation again, she answered
him instead.

When he had gone, she laughed. She said that she had pierced his heart and he would dream of her. It angered and upset me, and when I got back to the house I sank into my chair and burst into tears.

More and more, I enjoyed going to church and hearing Mr Weston's voice. I savoured the small smiles he gave me, and the passing glances. They gave me hope that we would become closer.

Soon after that, Rosalie became engaged to Sir Thomas Ashby. Her mother had planned it, but Rosalie liked the idea of becoming the mistress of Ashby Park. She would have a honeymoon abroad and many parties to attend. I knew that it was a bad idea, and that he wasn't right for her, but she just laughed.

During all this time, however, she still used every opportunity to see Mr Weston. She wanted to convince him that she really loved him. I could not believe anyone could behave in such a way.

During the six weeks of preparation before Miss Rosalie's wedding I continued to visit the villagers, always hoping to see Mr Weston. I had heard that he was soon leaving to go to another parish. Returning through the lanes and fields, I walked more slowly than usual, hoping that he would come

by. One day he did, carrying a bunch of bluebells, which he offered to me with a smile.

We walked and talked for a while, and he asked me about the books I liked to read. That small event gave me a pleasant evening and a night of happy dreams.

Chapter Seven

On the first of June, Miss Rosalie Murray became Lady Ashby. She looked beautiful in her wedding dress and was very excited as they left for their honeymoon in Europe.

A few days later I received a letter from home saying that my father was dying.

After gaining Mrs Murray's permission, I left for home.

But I was too late. My father had died.

My sister, Mary, wanted our mother to go and live with her. But Mamma was healthy and independent and didn't want to be looked after.

'I will look for a small house,' she said, 'where Agnes and I can take in a few young ladies to board and educate. What do you say, Agnes? Shall we run a small school?'

'I have a little money saved that we could use,' I said. I was quite excited at the idea.

A couple of weeks later, Mamma received a letter from her father.

7th September

Dear Lucy,

I have no doubt that you are sorry you married Richard Grey and have led an unhappy life as a result. If you will admit to this and say that you should have listened to my advice, then I will make a lady of you again and remember your daughters in my will.

Yours

Papa

She wrote straight back.

10th September

Father,

You are mistaken. I certainly do not regret the birth of my daughters. They have been the pride of my life and will be the comfort of my old age.

Nor do I regret the thirty years I spent with my husband and dearest friend.

I was made for him and he for me.

If our problems had been three times worse, I would still rejoice at having shared them with Richard.

Lucy

Mary and I were pleased with that, even though it meant that we would never meet him or have any money from him.

With sadness, we left the old house where I was born and the little village church where my father had been vicar. I left the desolate hills and the green woods, and went back to Horton Lodge. I gave six weeks' notice to Mrs Murray that I was leaving.

It was two weeks before I saw Mr Weston. He asked how my family were, and I told him of our plans for the school.

'Then you will be leaving here?' he asked.

'Yes, in a month,' I said.

'I expect you will be glad to leave,' he said.

'I shall miss the family,' I said. 'I have been here for two years. I shall miss Snap too, the little terrier that they gave me.' I didn't say that the person I would miss most would be him.

We walked together for a while. He never once spoke of love or gave any hint of any affection he felt for me. Still, I was happy. I enjoyed hearing him talk and being near him. There was so much I wanted to say to him, but I kept it to myself. It wasn't my way to be so bold.

Then came the last service in the church. I knew this might be the last time I heard his voice or saw his face. I almost melted into tears.

Outside, he came to me.

'I suppose you are going this week, Miss Grey?' he asked.

'Yes.'

'Then I bid you goodbye.' He held out his hand.

'Goodbye, Mr Weston.' Oh, how I struggled to say it calmly.

'We may meet again,' he said. 'Would that please you?'

'Oh, yes. I would be very glad if we did.'

I could not bear the thought of never seeing him again. I thought of him day and night, but no one saw my tears or heard my prayers.

Chapter Eight

I went home and joined Mamma in the house she had bought. We had three boarders and six day pupils, so I was kept busy. But I was always thinking of Mr Weston. Every time there was a knock on the door my heart raced. Whenever I received a letter, I opened it in restless excitement. I was disappointed when it wasn't from him.

Mamma had noticed that something was wrong. She thought the sea air would do me good. I smiled and tried to be more cheerful around her.

I did hear from Rosalie, who was now Lady Ashby. She invited me to spend some time with them in the holidays. She said that they had a baby girl, who was very sweet, but Rosalie was pleased she did not have to look after her. Sir Thomas

was disappointed that the baby was
not a boy.

I did visit and she was pleased
to show me her home. There was
a French poodle sitting on a silk
cushion, and many Italian paintings.

She told me about her family and all the other families I had known in the village.

Then I asked her about Mr Weston.

'Oh, he left Horton about a month ago,' she said. 'I don't know where he went.'

At last, she admitted that she had made a mistake in marrying Sir Thomas Ashby. She was very unhappy, although she was rich and her life seemed wonderful.

He was often away gambling and spending time with other women.

I suggested she might enjoy being with her little daughter, but I doubted she would take my advice.

I stayed for three days and then went back home.

Our house was one of a row of neat houses, with small gardens at the front. It was not near the sea, but I often enjoyed walking down to the

town and along the beach, especially
if the sea was a little rough.

I was on such a walk early one
morning, just as the church clock
struck a quarter to six.

I took off my shoes and enjoyed the feel of the sand between my toes as I walked along the beach. The bright sunshine was rising over the craggy cliffs.

There was a little breeze, and the waves came bounding to the shore, foaming and sparkling.

There was no one else around.
I was the first to walk on the
unbroken sand since the last tide
had wiped it smooth.

I sat on a rock and watched
as people began to stir. First the
grooms arrived to exercise their
horses, then the water cart came to
get water for the public baths. Soon
people came out for their morning
walk or swim.

I squinted into the sun. The

tide was coming in and seagulls screeched overhead.

Then I heard a snuffling sound and a dog came frisking and wriggling around my feet.

It was Snap, the wirehaired terrier that had been mine at the Murrays' home! I called his name and he leapt up into my arms. How had he come to be here?

'Your dog remembers you, Miss Grey,' said a voice I knew so well.

I turned, and there stood Mr Weston. I tried to be calm although my heart raced.

'I am the curate in Fensworth,' he said. 'Just two miles from here.'

I couldn't believe it! He had been so close for all these weeks.

We stood up and began to walk up towards the road. He offered me his arm and I took it. The closeness of him took my breath away.

'I have looked for you here,' he said. 'Snap and I often walk on the beach, but we have never seen you. I asked if I could have him when you left.'

My heart lifted with joy.

'I would like to meet your mother,' he said.

'Then come tomorrow,' I said, as we parted. I watched as he strolled away with Snap at his heels.

Chapter Nine

I couldn't wait for the next day. He arrived about noon and I was pleased that Mamma and him seemed to get on straight away.

After that, he often called on us. Eventually we called each other by our first names.

One evening he asked my mother if he could take me for a walk to Ramsey Hill. There was a wonderful view at the top.

When we were halfway up the hill he said, 'My house is so lonely, Agnes. Although I know several ladies in this town, there is only one person who would suit me as a companion, and that is you.'

He laid his hand on my arm
and said, 'It's not my way to talk
about my feelings. A single word
or glance from me means so much
more. But I want to know if you
will be my wife.'

My heart quickened. 'But Mamma ...'

'I spoke to her already while you were getting your coat. I have her consent. Do you love me?'

'Yes,' I said.

I shall never forget that glorious summer evening on that hill. We watched the sunset mirrored in the water below us. Our hearts were so full of happiness and love that we couldn't speak.

A few weeks later, I became Mrs Edward Weston. Now we have three children – Edward, Agnes and Mary.

We have little money, but it is enough for us. More importantly, we have a lot of love.

On the coach journey, we passed green, reedy swamps, flat fields and trees. It rained heavily. Finally, through the starless night, I saw the lights of Brussels.

Penniless and rejected by his cruel brother, William Crimsworth travels to Belgium to start a new life. He becomes a professor and grows close to a young teacher he starts tutoring. But the girls in his class are determined to make trouble and his new friend suddenly leaves the school without a word …